Illustrated by Amanda Welch

To my parents, with love

Other Sammy stories by Odette Elliott

Under Sammy's Bed
Sammy Goes Flying
Sammy and the Telly

Scholastic Children's Books,
Scholastic Publications Ltd,
7-9 Pratt Street, London NW1 OAE, UK

Scholastic Inc.,
555 Broadway, New York, NY 10012-3999, USA

Scholastic Canada Ltd,
123 Newkirk Road, Richmond Hill,
Ontario, Canada L4C 3G5

Ashton Scholastic Pty Ltd,
PO Box 579, Gosford, New South Wales,
Australia

Ashton Scholastic Ltd,
Private Bag 92801, Penrose, Auckland,
New Zealand

First published in hardback by Scholastic Publications Ltd, 1992
This edition published 1994

ISBN: 0 590 55685 1

Typeset by Rapid Reprographics
Printed in Hong Kong by Paramount Printing Group Ltd

10 9 8 7 6 5 4 3 2 1

Sammy woke up early on the morning of Christmas Eve. The clock struck six times. His big brother Tony was asleep.

"No stocking yet," Sammy said to Teddy. "I *wish* it was Christmas Day!"

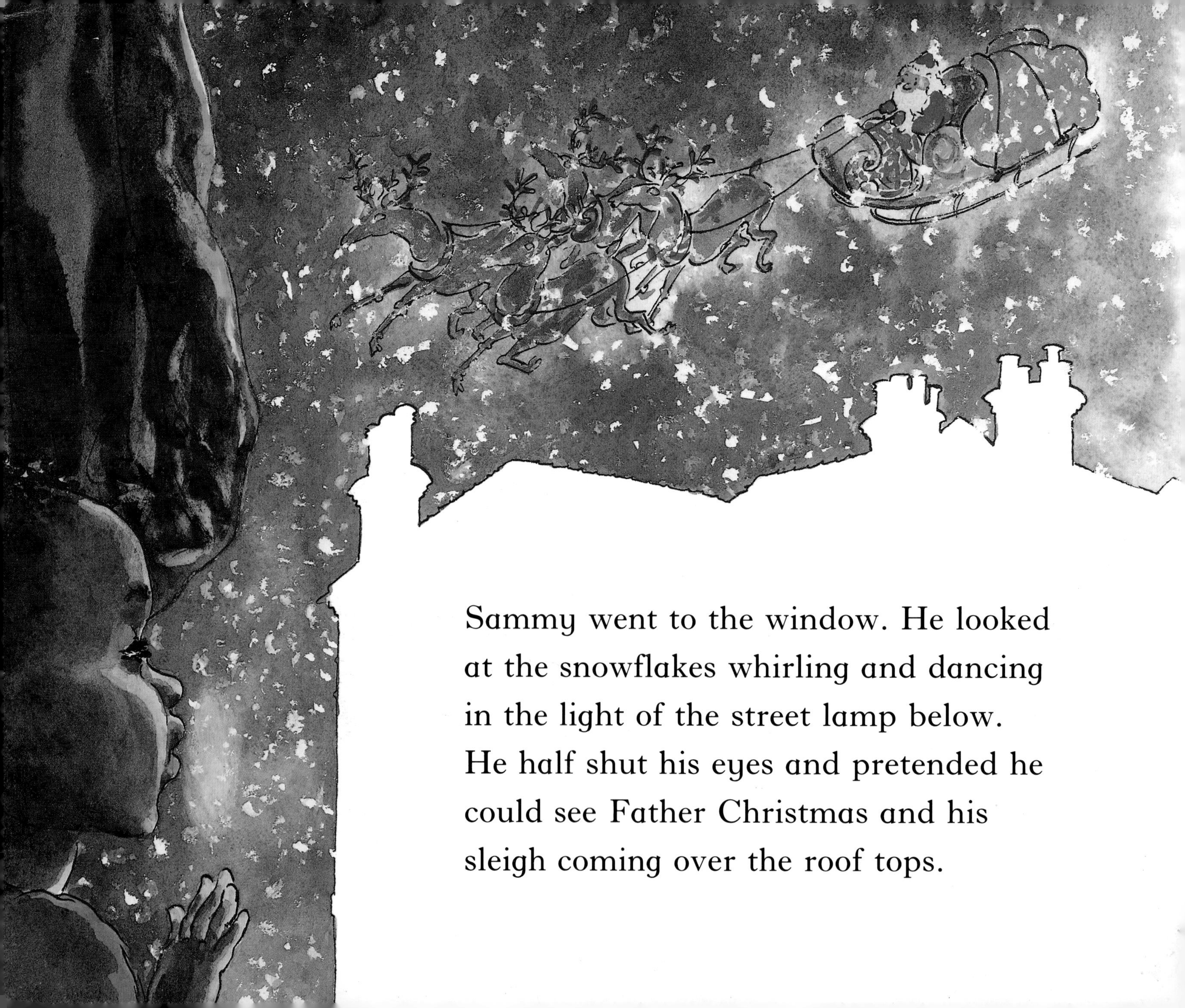

Sammy went to the window. He looked at the snowflakes whirling and dancing in the light of the street lamp below. He half shut his eyes and pretended he could see Father Christmas and his sleigh coming over the roof tops.

Then he
opened his eyes.
"I know," Sammy
said, "Let's go downstairs
and see the tree. I hope the
decorations haven't fallen off."

The Christmas tree looked lovely. The coloured balls shone and the tinsel sparkled. "Pretty!" said Sammy. The boxes for the decorations were still in the room. Sammy picked up the little white bits of packing material and threw them in the air.

"Look, Teddy! Snow! You sit in the box. Let's pretend it's your sledge."
The sledge went up hill and down and round corners fast.

Suddenly Sammy heard the clock strike eight.
Mum came in. "Sammy!" she said. "I didn't hear you getting up. What *is* all that mess?"
"It's not mess. It's snow at the North Pole – and Teddy is Santa coming in his sleigh," said Sammy.

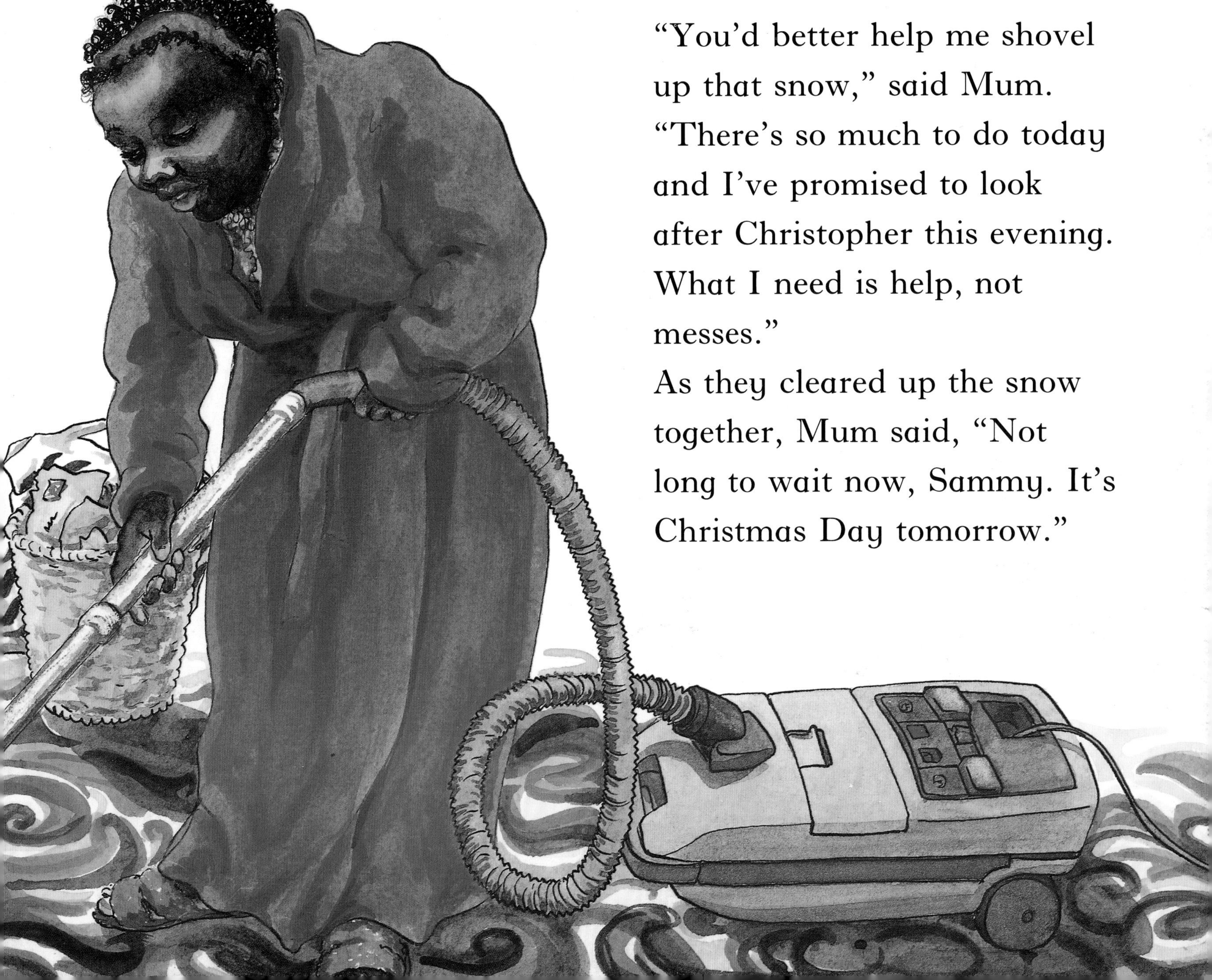

"You'd better help me shovel
up that snow," said Mum.
"There's so much to do today
and I've promised to look
after Christopher this evening.
What I need is help, not
messes."
As they cleared up the snow
together, Mum said, "Not
long to wait now, Sammy. It's
Christmas Day tomorrow."

When the clock struck ten, Sammy and his sisters, Melissa and Christine, went shopping with Dad.
Sammy had to carry the Christmas crackers. He shut his eyes and bumped into a pile of sprouts.
"Look where you're going!" Dad said.
"I can't," said Sammy. "I'm being a monster and he doesn't have any eyes."
"Try being a helpful monster, then, and help to pick these up," said Dad.

After lunch Sammy heard
the clock strike two. “Teddy
wants it to be Christmas
Day,” he said.
“It will be soon,” said Tony.
“Would anyone like to help
make paper chains?” “Me!”
said Melissa and Christine.
“And me!” said Sammy.
They all went to the corner
shop to buy the packets of
paper strips for paper chains.

DOGS NOT ALLOWED
WHITE CHRISTMAS ROAD & RAIL CHAOS

Sammy couldn't make
his chains stick together.
He looked for something
else to do.
"I'll make something *much*
better," he said, sprinkling
glitter and glue over a
piece of card.

He got glitter all over the carpet.

but he thought it looked pretty –
like the Christmas lights in town.

When Mum saw it she said, “Oh, Sammy!
Not another mess.”
“It’s not a mess. It’s coloured stars,”
he said. It took Sammy such a
long time to clear up the
coloured stars, that he thought
it must be nearly Christmas
Day.
He heard the clock, but
it only struck four.

He went into the kitchen.
"Isn't it ever going to be Christmas Day?" he asked.
"Yes, in a few hours. Why don't you go and play in your bedroom?" Dad suggested.
"I can't! Tony says he's wrapping presents and he won't let me in."
Just then Tony came out of the bedroom with a large parcel. "Is that for me?" Sammy asked.

Then the front door bell rang and Mrs. Jones from next door stood there with Christopher.
"Christopher's fast asleep. He should be quiet for a long time," she said.
"Come in," said Mum. "He can go in Sammy and Tony's room while he's sleeping."
Sammy and Teddy couldn't think what to do. They went and sat in the bedroom and looked at Christopher.
When the clock struck six Christopher woke up and cried. His eyes filled with big tears and he opened his mouth and screamed.

"Can someone see
what's the matter
with Christopher?"
Mum called out.

"I'm on the phone,"
said Dad.

“We’re wrapping presents,”
said Melissa and Christine.

“I’m putting up paper
chains,” said Tony.

"I will!" said Sammy. "I'll HELP."
Sammy looked at the toys in his toy box. He pulled out a drum, then a caterpillar with coloured legs.
Christopher stopped crying. Then Sammy took out a dog with floppy ears and a clown. Sammy made the clown dance and Christopher laughed.
"I know. Let's put all the toys out and pretend it's Santa's workshop at the North Pole," said Sammy.
"That's where he gets all the Christmas presents ready for the children. We'll be his helpers."

not
Pol

The helpers at Santa's workshop laughed a lot and worked very hard.

Sammy and Christopher and Teddy were so busy that they did not hear Christopher's mother come to collect him. "What a good boy you are!" Christopher's mother said to Sammy.

All the family came to see what Sammy had done. He showed them the pretend workshop. They had to be careful where to put their feet.

"It isn't a mess this time, Mum," Sammy said.
"It's a HELP!"
"It's a lovely help!" said Mum.
At that moment the clock struck eight.
"Now I can hang up my stocking,
can't I?" said Sammy.
"Yes," said Mum.
"Happy Christmas, Teddy!" Sammy
whispered.